Dedication

For my youngest daughter, Mollie, whose love of gymnastics as a young girl was the inspiration for this novel. "Maddie," the main character, has your inner strength, unwillingness to give up in the face of challenges, and passion for life. These admirable qualities are the ones that make Olympic gymnastic stars like Simone Biles, Gabby Douglas, Laurie Hernandez, Madison Kocan, and Aly Raisman heroes for young, aspiring athletes everywhere!

TABLE OF CONTENTS

I.

MADDIE

My name is Maddie Hoffman. For those of you who don't know me, I am a nine-year-old "Gymnastics Superstar." You're probably thinking that I'm bragging, but it's really true! Gymnastics Superstars is the name of the program I attend at the Harrison Street Gym every Tuesday and Thursday afternoon.

I just love gymnastics! From the time I was very young, my favorite things to do were handstands, cartwheels, rope climbing, swinging on monkey bars, and tumbling on mats. My older siblings—Brayden, Rebecca, and Jason, who are triplets—would often join me, but none of them felt about gymnastics the way I did. Mom always said they didn't have the same "passion" as me...but more about them later.

Now that I am nine, I know that "passion" means that I can't live without gymnastics. So when I turned four, Mom enrolled me in a one-hour beginners class in the Harrison Street Superstar Recreational Gymnastics Program. I was so happy!

I don't really remember much about that time, but Mom told me that I could never wait for my Wednesday afternoon gymnastics class. She tells everyone the same embarrassing

1

story over and over again about how upset I would get when I couldn't go to gymnastics. Every morning I would ask her, "Is today Wednesday?" When she would answer, "No," I would cross my arms on my chest, pull my eyebrows together, close my lips tightly, and refuse to move. Both Mom and Dad called this "the Maddie look." No matter what they did to try and persuade me to get dressed for school, I would not budge. Getting me to change my mind was not easy because I was so stubborn.

But Mom did not give up. Since she was an elementary school teacher, she knew how to deal with angry children. Mom came up with a pretty cool idea to solve the problem, although I've never told her I thought it was good. She made a special gymnastics countdown chart with boxes for all the days of the week. When I woke up every morning except Wednesday, I would get to color each box blue to show that I was sad that I wasn't going to gymnastics that day. On Wednesdays, I colored the box red, my very favorite color. I had no problem getting to school on time when I knew that Mom was taking me to the Harrison Street Gym after school was over.

Sunday	Monday	Tuesday	Wednesday	Thursday	Friday	Saturday

Even though it was a long time ago, I do remember Mom picking me up at preschool to go to my gymnastics class. When I got in our car, the first thing I saw was my really cool gymnastics bag with its red hearts and my name, "Maddie," printed in red. Inside the bag was my favorite red leotard and a yummy snack.

It has been pretty much the same routine since I was four. Mom always picks me up after school and takes me to prac-tice. The only differences are that I now go to gymnastics twice a week on Tuesdays and Thursdays, and the snacks aren't so good anymore. Now that I am nine and a serious gymnast, I have to think about my body. Mom only lets me have healthy snacks. Yogurt, a banana, carrot sticks...boring! She should see what the other kids bring to the gym!

But I get it! I'm no longer a beginner. I'm in the most advanced recreational gymnastics class, where I just earned my seventh star. This is the final star of the Superstars program—the Gold! I am so excited because I can now try out for Team, and if I pass the test, I will become a member of USAG. That's "USA Gymnastics." This means that I will get to compete at meets all over.

I am not sure how excited Mom and Dad are about this. If I make Team, it means many more hours at the gym after school and on weekends. I could have earned my Gold star and tried out for Team a long time ago, but Mom and Dad didn't want me spending so much time at the gym. So I know they are not going to be happy with this big change in my schedule, but I won't mind it at all!

Now I have to get ready for the Spring All Around Meet. Although this meet is really just a performance for all gym-

nasts in the Recreational Program to show off their skills for their parents, it is also my chance to try out for Team. All the coaches will be there to decide if I'm ready for competitive gymnastics. I think I am because I have done really well in competitions we have had with other Advanced Recreational groups. But all the coaches keep telling us that the competitions we have had so far are just "practice" so we get to know what it's like to really compete. Since competition in USA Gymnastics is at a much higher level, the test will be very hard!

I have to do one "compulsory routine" on the balance beam, uneven bars, or floor. This is a basic set of skills that everyone who competes is required to do. Every gymnast gets the same music and same skills. Since I only have to do one, I'm going to do floor because I love to tumble. It sounds easy, but it really isn't. The judges subtract points for the tiniest mistakes! To make things even harder, I have to add one "optional" skill to my routine. I like the idea that I get to choose one skill that I love and put it in my routine wherever I want. But it would be so much easier to just do the compulsory routine without any changes.

I'm kind of nervous, but I know I'm tough…and stubborn like Mom and Dad say. But I think stubborn can be a good thing. With my toughness, my stubbornness, and my passion for gymnastics, how can I lose? The Meet is just 2½ weeks away. I have a lot of work to do!

2.

AFTER SCHOOL ANTICS

Nine-year-old Maddie Hoffman sat impatiently in her Grade 4 math class staring at the clock through her shiny red eyeglasses. Although math was her favorite subject, Maddie could not pay attention.

Five minutes to go, she thought to herself.

Counting the seconds and minutes in her head, the 3:30 PM bell finally rang. Maddie could not leave school fast enough. As all the upper elementary students at Royal Palm Academy ran to their lockers and then to the buses or carpool line, Maddie was ahead of them of all. Today was Thursday, and that meant gymnastics practice. Running out the exit doors with her long, brown hair flying in the wind, Maddie made a beeline for her mother's car. Spotting the family minivan in front of the carpool line, Maddie smiled. *Mom never disappoints me on gym days,* she thought to herself.

"Hi, Mom," Maddie said. "Let's go. I don't want to be late for practice."

"No, Maddie. Not yet," Mrs. Hoffman responded. "You know we have to wait for your brothers and sister.

Brayden, Rebecca, and Jason were Maddie's eleven-year-old fraternal triplet siblings who didn't look anything alike.

Where Brayden had brown hair, blue eyes, and wore glasses, Jason was shorter and skinnier, with brown hair and brown eyes. Rebecca was also skinny, with curly red hair, brown eyes, and lots of freckles. The two boys were in sixth grade at Royal Palm Academy, but Rebecca was one year behind in fifth grade. This was because of difficulties she'd had when she was younger with learning to read and write.

"Why can't they be on time?" Maddie asked. "They're just doing this to make me mad. Can't you take me and then come back for the boys and Rebecca? Please, Mom!" Maddie pleaded. "You know how important practice is to me. I have got to make Team. I've worked so hard on my routine, but I have so much more to do. I just have to get there!"

Mrs. Hoffman sighed. Having had this same conversation with Maddie every time she went to after school gymnastics, she patiently explained, "Maddie, school just ended. Brayden, Rebecca, and Jason will be here. You know that Rebecca and the boys' classes are further away from the exit than your fourth grade class. We need to wait for them. Besides…have you ever been late to practice?"

Maddie refused to respond. Although she realized her mother was right, she didn't want to admit it. "Why can't they walk faster?" she mumbled to herself, as she French-braided her hair. Maddie knew that her long, brown hair needed to be pulled back tightly whenever she went to practice.

Before Maddie could get angrier, Brayden yanked the front door open.

"Why does Maddie get to sit in front?" he complained. "Just because she gets out of school first doesn't mean she gets shotgun!"

"Not to worry, Brayden," Mrs. Hoffman responded. "After we drop Maddie off at gymnastics, you can switch to the front seat."

"That's not fair!" Jason said. "He had the front seat yesterday. It's my turn."

"When are you kids going to stop fighting about who gets the front seat? Do we need to go back to the *Daily Shotgun Chart*?" Mrs. Hoffman asked in an annoyed tone.

"That chart is for babies!" Rebecca yelled from the back of the van. "Why can't you boys grow up?"

"Enough already!" Mrs. Hoffman shouted. "Maddie has the front seat now and Brayden later. That's it. I don't want to hear another word about shotgun."

The foursome got quiet. They knew how far they could push their mother and didn't want to take any chances of getting punished for something as dumb as fights for shotgun.

For the rest of the ride to the gym, the triplets sat quietly in the back while Mrs. Hoffman quizzed Maddie on her spelling words for her weekly Friday spelling test. When they pulled up to the gym, Maddie grabbed her gym bag and snack and hopped out.

"Bye, Mom!" she said, as she began to run into the gym.

"Wait, Maddie!" Mrs. Hoffman called after her. "Remember that Daddy is picking you up, and you need to be ready on time. You have a lot to do when you come home… dinner, bath, and studying for your Social Studies test."

"I know, Mom," Maddie said, sounding annoyed. "Have I ever gotten anything but an 'A' on my Social Studies tests?"

Maddie ran off without waiting for her mother to answer. With a sigh, Mrs. Hoffman pulled out of the parking lot and began to think about Maddie. *How is she going to keep up with both school and gymnastics if she really does make Team? Now she's at the gym two days a week for six hours. Team will be three days a week for nine hours plus weekend competitions! Will this be too much for her?*

This was a question she did not have a chance to think about for too long. When she pulled into the driveway, the triplets piled out and ran into the house. As they flopped down on the couch and turned on the television, they were stopped in their tracks by their mother.

"Homework first before anything else!" she ordered. "Get your snacks and then upstairs to your own rooms."

"Aw, Mom!" they shouted in unison.

"You know the rules. No TV, video games, iPad, or cell phones until homework is finished."

As they slowly climbed the stairs, Brayden whined, "It's not fair. Maddie gets to go to gymnastics, but we have to do homework."

"No problem," Jason responded. "When we're watching TV later on and chilling out, Maddie will be in her room doing homework."

With smiles on their faces, Jason, Rebecca, and Brayden continued their march upstairs.

"Let's get this over with quick!"

❧

While the triplets worked on their homework, Mrs. Hoffman went to the den to prepare lesson plans for the fifth grade class she taught at a nearby elementary school. As she got to work, she could hear her children's upstairs conversations on the intercom. Listening to their chatter about Maddie, she began to remember back to the time when her four-year-old daughter began gymnastics at the Harrison Street Gym. Every Wednesday, Maddie would attend a one hour beginner's class. Although she was the youngest in a group of four-, five-, and six-years-olds, she always stood out from the rest. Mrs. Hoffman smiled as she pictured Maddie with her big brown eyes shining through her red eyeglasses, her swinging braids, and little red leotard. *She really was cute and knew how to charm her coaches,* she thought to herself.

Being cute, however, was not enough. From her very first class, the coaches could see that Maddie was going to be an excellent gymnast. Not only did she know how to follow directions well, but she learned each new skill easily and much more quickly than any of the other children in her group. She was so good that she was able to earn her first three stars—Red, Orange, and Yellow—in her first eight-week session of the Superstars program. Mrs. Hoffman remembered the coaches bragging to her that none of their gymnasts had ever done that before! With each new star, Maddie moved to a new level and a more advanced class. Although each new level required that Maddie spend a lot more time at the gym, she didn't mind. Gymnastics was her passion...

"Passion!" Mrs. Hoffman blurted. Roused from her flashback into Maddie's past, Mrs. Hoffman stood up. "Yes! Gymnastics is Maddie's passion!" Thinking back about Maddie made her realize how important gymnastics was to her daughter. "If competition is what Maddie wants, then we need to be there for her no matter how difficult it may be!"

Mrs. Hoffman's spoken thoughts were interrupted when Jason barged into the den. "Mom! Who are you talking to?" he asked.

With an embarrassed look on her face, Mrs. Hoffman answered, "Uh, uh, nobody, Jason." Quickly changing the subject, she said, "Did you finish your homework?"

"Of course!" Jason replied. "I'm going to watch TV." Running out of the den, Jason mumbled to himself, "First one done! The remote is mine!"

3.

PROBLEMS AT PRACTICE

While the Hoffman triplets were rushing to finish their homework, Maddie was hard at work at the gym. With her warm-up exercises almost done, Maddie felt relief. Although she couldn't wait to get back to practicing her routine, she knew that warm-up was something every gymnast had to do. Her coaches called it "conditioning." This meant that you had to do lots of exercises to strengthen all the muscles in your body no matter if you were in a beginner Superstars class or a member of Team.

As Maddie practiced her splits, she could hear Coach Deb's voice in her head. *You have to stretch your muscles, girls. Your muscles are super tight. Every time you stretch them, they open a little bit more and then a little bit more. The more you stretch them out, your splits will get bigger and closer to the ground....*

"Yes!" shouted Maddie. "I did it, Coach! Did you see me? My splits are getting better and better! Can I now work on my routine?"

"Not yet, Maddie. Great splits, but you still need more stretching. You know how important it is to warm up your muscles and loosen your joints."

4.

MADDIE'S SURPRISE PLAN

"Hi, Maddie," Dr. Hoffman said as she climbed in the front seat. "How's my little girl doing?"

"I'm not your little girl! I'm nine years old, and I don't want to talk to you!" Maddie snapped.

"What's wrong?" Dr. Hoffman asked. "Did something happen at practice?"

"I said I don't want to talk. Leave me alone!"

Dr. Hoffman decided it was best to do just that. Silence filled the car.

Upon arriving home, Maddie jumped out of the car and ran into the house. As she dropped her gym bag on the family room floor and started to run upstairs, her mother stopped her.

"Wait, Maddie! You know the rules. Your gym bag belongs in your room. Take it upstairs, and then come downstairs for dinner. I have your plate warming in the oven."

Maddie turned around and grabbed her gym bag. Running up the stairs, she shouted, "I don't want dinner. I'm not hungry. Just leave me alone!" With these final words, Maddie slammed her bedroom door.

"What happened, Scott?" Mrs. Hoffman asked her husband.

"I don't know. Maddie refused to talk to me the whole car ride home. You know how she gets when she is upset," Dr. Hoffman answered.

"Yeah, we all know!" Brayden said, as he looked up from the family room couch where he and his siblings were watching TV. "She gets the *Maddie Look*. You don't want to mess with her when she gets that way!"

"Let me handle Maddie," Jason offered. "I know how to deal with her. When she cools down, I'll talk to her."

"Thanks, but no thanks, Jason," Mrs. Hoffman said firmly. "Dad and I will deal with Maddie." Mrs. Hoffman knew that Jason loved to tease and that Rebecca and Brayden would join in. "You and your siblings need to stay out of this. Do you understand? I'm sure you'd all like to continue watching TV rather than be punished for interfering in Maddie's business."

Although they'd much prefer to bother their sister, the triplets kept quiet. It just wasn't worth the risk of losing their TV privileges.

Thirty minutes later, Dr. and Mrs. Hoffman knocked on Maddie's door.

"Come in," Maddie said quietly.

Carrying a food tray filled with a steaming hot plate of spaghetti and meatballs, one of Maddie's favorites, her mother entered first, followed by her father. Maddie was sitting on her bed with her Social Studies text and notebook open. Surrounding her were stuffed animals and her favorite doll. Actually named Maddie, the doll looked just like Maddie when she was a little girl, with braids and red glasses.

"Maddie, what happened at the gym today?" Mrs. Hoffman asked.

"We know you're upset, but talking about it may help you feel better," Dr. Hoffman added.

Maddie's eyes filled with tears. As hard as she tried not to cry, she could not hold back her tears. Cuddled in her father's arms, Maddie told them everything that happened with Maya and Jenny and all the mistakes she'd made doing her routine.

"Maya and Jenny were so mean to me! I messed up my routine because of them. I'm never gonna make Team if they keep bothering me," Maddie said, crying.

"We know how hard you're working to make Team," Dr. Hoffman said softly. "We're very proud of everything you have accomplished, so we understand why you're upset."

"But what can I do?" Maddie asked.

"Well…maybe the three of us can put our heads together and figure out a solution," Mrs. Hoffman answered. "But you need to take the lead, Maddie. Not only are you smart, but you know Maya and Jenny a lot better than we do."

"Why do you think these girls are being mean to you?" Dr. Hoffman asked.

Maddie thought for a few seconds. "I guess it's because they're angry that they haven't gotten their Gold Stars. Maybe they're jealous because I'm a year younger than them."

"I think you're right!" Mrs. Hoffman said. "They are jealous." She paused and then asked, "Do you remember some of the things you learned in the *Stomp Out Bullying* program at school?"

"Why? Do you think Maya and Jenny are bullies?" Maddie asked.

"I'm not sure they're bullies yet, but the way they acted towards you is bullying in the making," her mother answered.

"Well…I do remember some of the things they taught us. They said that bullies look for their victims' weak spots and will keep bothering them because they know they're afraid. They told us that victims have to stop showing fear, or the bullies will continue to hurt them."

"That's right, Maddie," Dr. Hoffman said. "So how can you use what you learned about bullies to help you with Maya and Jenny?"

"Maybe I need to show Maya and Jenny that I'm not afraid of them."

Mrs. Hoffman nodded her head. "I agree. You can't show fear, but how are you going to stop them from bothering you?"

"If I could get them to stop being jealous of me, maybe they'd leave me alone," Maddie answered. "In *Stomp Out Bullying*, they said we need to throw bullies off guard by saying or doing something the bully wouldn't expect. What can I do that would surprise them?"

"Maybe you need to think about some of the things that Maya and Jenny do well in gymnastics?" her mother responded.

Maddie sat quietly thinking to herself. *Why does Mom care about what they do well? They aren't good at anything!* As she thought a little more, she realized that wasn't true.

"So what do you think, Maddie?" Dr. Hoffman asked.

"Well…I have to admit that Maya really does good splits. I think that's why she thought I was bragging about my splits. And Katie is great at round-offs." Maddie paused for a few seconds, and then an idea suddenly popped into her head. "I've got it! I'm going to compliment Maya and Jenny on the things they are good at."

"Great idea!" Mrs. Hoffman said.

"When I go to practice on Sunday, I'm going to throw them off guard just like I was taught. After warm-up, I'm going to tell them that I've been thinking about what they said on Thursday and realized that they're just as good at gymnastics as me. Then I'll tell Maya how good she is at splits, and Katie about how I wish I could do round-offs like she does. Maybe I can even ask them to give me some advice on how I can improve my routine. Do you think that will work?" Maddie asked.

"I think it's great," Dr. Hoffman answered. "We can't be sure it'll work, but it's worth a shot. Go for it, Maddie Girl!"

"In the meantime, your meatballs and spaghetti are asking for you," her mother teased. "Eat your dinner, finish your homework, and take a bath. It's getting late." Mrs. Hoffman started to walk out of Maddie's room but then turned around. "And make sure to eat your dinner at your desk. I better not find any meatball or spaghetti stains on your bed!"

"Yes, Mom," Maddie said, with a smile on her face. "I know the rules!"

5.

MADDIE

*T*oday is Sunday. That means I have two weeks to nail my routine before I have to try out for Team. Up until this past Thursday, when Maya and Katie started bothering me, I was really excited about performing my routine at the Meet. Even though I was nervous, I thought I'd be okay. Now I am not so sure. Even though Mom and Dad gave me a pep talk and made me feel a lot better about myself, I am still kinda scared to go to practice today.

Even my brother Jason says that Maya and Jenny are "messing with my head." Although he wasn't supposed to butt into my business, Jason came and listened at the door when Mom and  Dad were talking to me. I should be mad at him, but I'm not.

 He said that I need to act cool like him. "Be nice but tough!" Those are the words he always repeats.

That's actually how I act with my cat, Lucky. Lucky weighs 26 pounds and likes to play mind games with anyone who's scared of him. He just loves to jump out at *people and swipe at them. But he doesn't do that to me because I'm not afraid, and Lucky knows I'm boss!*

So that's it. I'm not going to let Maya and Jenny play mind games with me! It's time to go to practice and face them. Wish me luck!

What Do You Think?

What will happen when Maddie goes to gym practice on Sunday?
(Place an "X" next to your prediction below.)

☐ Maddie will say nice things to Maya and Jenny, become their friend, and work together with them in the gym.

☐ Maddie will say nice things to Maya and Jenny, but they continue to bully her, which makes her ruin her routine.

☐ Maddie will avoid Maya and Jenny because she is too scared. The girls continue to bully her, which makes her ruin her routine.

☐ Maddie continues to get bullied after she says nice things to Maya and Jenny, but she doesn't let it ruin her routine.

☐ Other _____

Explain why you made your prediction above:

_____
_____
_____
_____
_____
_____
_____

6.

SUNDAY MORNING PRACTICE

When Maddie arrived at the gym, she went to the locker room where Katie was waiting for her.

"Maddie!" Katie whispered. "Maya and Jenny are already in the warm-up area giggling to each other. They didn't know I could hear them talking about you. What are you going to do?"

"I've got a plan. Mom and Dad helped me figure it out. I'm not sure it's gonna work, but I have to try something! When we finish warm-up, just stay with me."

"What are you going to do, Maddie? I don't want to get in any trouble two weeks before Team tryout."

"Don't worry, Katie. If anything goes wrong, I'll take the blame. I just need my best friend there with me," Maddie said, pleading with her.

With a big smile on her face, Katie said, "Okay, Maddie. You're my best friend, too. Let's go."

❧

Warm-up exercises moved quickly. As all the girls were anxious to get through conditioning, they followed Coach Deb's commands without a moan or groan.

"Great workout, girls!" Coach shouted. "Maddie and Jenny to the floor and beam. The rest of you, alternate between the bars and vault. Let's go!"

When the Advanced class left the warm-up area, Maya and Jenny lagged behind and began to follow Maddie and Katie. Feeling their presence behind her, Maddie quickly turned around and walked right up to Maya and Jenny. Katie was right by her side.

You can do this! Maddie thought to herself. *Be nice but tough!*

"Hi, girls!" Maddie said, with a big smile on her face. "I'm so glad you're here. I wanted to talk to you."

Maya and Jenny looked at each other with surprise in their eyes, but before they could say anything, Maddie continued talking.

"I was thinking about what happened on Thursday and realized that I haven't been fair to you. All of us in Advanced are really good, but each of us has something we do the best. Like you, Maya. You do the best splits! And Jenny, your round-offs are amazing!" Maddie paused. Looking at Katie, she added, "And you, Katie, do the best beam dismounts! I guess that's why you're doing a beam routine at the Meet."

"And what about you, Maddie?" Katie jumped in. "No one does back handsprings like you!"

Maya and Jenny were shocked. They couldn't believe Maddie was being so nice to them after the things they had said about her. They were speechless. So Maddie continued to talk.

"Since the two you are so good at splits and round-offs, I was wondering if you wouldn't mind helping me with my routine after you finish working on the bars and vault. I'm sure Coach would let you. She's always saying we need to work together as a team."

"And I could use some help, too, with my beam routine," Katie added.

Maya and Jenny did not know what to say.

How can we be mean to Maddie when she's saying nice things to us? Maya thought to herself. *I better say something!* Maya took a deep breath and swallowed hard.

"Sure, Maddie! Jenny and I are happy to help you and Katie. We'll go ask Coach to see if it's okay. Come on, Jenny," Maya called. As they started to run off, Jenny stopped. She turned around towards Maddie and Katie and shouted, "We think you're really good, too!"

Maddie beamed. "It worked!" she whispered to Katie. "I can't believe it! I didn't show how scared I was. I was nice but tough, just like my brother Jason told me to be, and it worked!"

"You were amazing, Maddie!" Katie said.

"We 'Superstars' really rock!" Maddie said to Katie. "We've got routines to ace. Let's get to work!"

7.

VICTORY CELEBRATION

When Maddie finished practice on Sunday, she really felt like a superstar and couldn't wait to tell her parents everything that happened. Not only had everything worked out great with Maya and Jenny, but she'd also performed her routine well with some helpful hints from her two new friends.

Maddie exited the gym to find the entire Hoffman family waiting for her in the minivan. Even Papa Max, her grandfather, was there. As she opened the door, Mrs. Hoffman asked, "How did it go, Maddie?" But she didn't really need to ask the question. The beaming smile on Maddie's face said it all.

"The plan worked!' she shouted. "I can't believe how easy it was. I was nice but tough to Maya and Jenny, and I wasn't scared at all!"

"Nice but tough?" Jason asked, with a smirk on his face. "I wonder where you've heard that before?"

Maddie ignored Jason. "The best part," she continued, "is that I didn't make any mistakes on my routine, and Maya and Jenny actually helped me! I'm so happy! Thanks, Mom and Dad!"

"No thanks, needed," Dr. Hoffman said. "You figured this one out all on your own. Mom and I didn't come up with the plan. You did, Maddie! Congratulations!"

"That's my Maddie!" Papa Max said, beaming.

Suddenly, Maddie focused on her siblings. "Why are all of **them** in the car?" she asked. "They never want to leave home on Sunday. Where are we going?"

"How about a family lunch at Jaxson's ice cream parlor to celebrate your victory?" Mrs. Hoffman asked.

"Wow! Can't say no to that!" Maddie answered. "Could this day get any better?"

Yes, it did! Lunch at Jaxson's was incredible, with Maddie eating all her favorites—hamburger with fries, Coca Cola, and a hot fudge sundae with chocolate chip ice cream. And the best part of it all was that her mother did not say one word about her not making healthy food choices.

At home, Maddie had no homework to complete for Monday. Since her brothers were outside playing basketball, and Rebecca was in her room doing homework, Maddie took advantage of the quiet. With her headphones on, she stretched out on the family room leather couch and listened to her favorite music. As she drifted off to sleep, she thought to herself, *My last chance to veg out before the Meet!*

8.

BACK ON TRACK

Just like Sunday, practice the following week went smoothly. On Tuesday and Thursday, the Advanced Recreational class moved quickly through their warm-up, followed by rotations on beam, bars, vault, and floor. The girls then rehearsed their group floor routine, which would be performed at the Meet. As they were the most advanced group, their routine would be the finale and the most spectacular presentation.

Although Maddie and Katie loved rehearsing this final act for the Meet, they were happy when Coach gave them the go-ahead to practice their individual routines. As Coach Deb watched, Maddie moved effortlessly through each skill in her compulsory routine: *straddle jump, front handspring, back extension roll, split leap, back walkover, and round-off back handspring.* Even her optional skill, *a back tuck* was done perfectly.

Katie's compulsory routine on the beam was also good. She aced each *cartwheel, split leap, handstand, split jump, and side handstand* as well as her optional skill—*a back walkover.*

As Maddie and Katie practiced their routines throughout the week, Maya and Jenny were there to give them help.

When practice was over on Thursday, both Maddie and Katie had to admit that their classmates' suggestions with splits and round-offs really helped them improve their routines.

"I can't believe how good our routines are getting!" Katie said quietly to Maddie, as they packed up their gym bags. "I know I shouldn't brag, but we didn't make any mistakes this week."

"I can't believe it, either," Maddie agreed. "But Coach Deb always says that we're gonna make mistakes no matter how good we are and that mistakes help us get better than before!"

With those final words, Maddie left the gym. Climbing into her mother's minivan, she thought to herself, *I know it's okay to make mistakes, but I hope I don't make any big ones before the Meet! Ten days to go...*

What Do You Think?

Will Maddie or Katie make any mistakes in the final week before the Meet? What do you think will happen to each of them? (Make your predictions below.)

Maddie

_____

_____

_____

_____

_____

_____

_____

_____

_____

Katie

_____

_____

_____

_____

_____

_____

_____

_____

_____

9.

TGIF...THANK GOD IT'S FRIDAY!

Friday dawned and was greeted with big smiles by the Hoffman foursome. Where the triplets Brayden, Rebecca, and Jason looked forward to two days of freedom from school, Maddie couldn't wait for gymnastic practice on Sunday. As they all piled into the car at the end of the school day, Jason shouted, "Let's get going, Mom! We need to get home right away."

"Yeah," said Brayden. "All the guys are coming over. We've got football and basketball games planned all weekend."

"Great!" Rebecca said.

"Why do you think it's great?" Jason asked. "You're not invited."

"Do you think I want to play football and basketball with you and your creepy friends? Not! I'll have the TV all to myself."

"Not all to yourself. What about me?" Maddie said. "I'll be there, too!"

"Really?" Mrs. Hoffman said. "You'll be in the gym all day Sunday, so no TV until your homework is done."

"No problem, Mom," Maddie said. "I don't mind doing homework on Saturday—"

"What's wrong with you?" Brayden said, interrupting. "Who wants to do homework on Saturday? Did your brain cells get scrambled when you were standing on your head?"

"Brayden's right," Jason added. "You have been such a nerd ever since you won the 'All About Me' writing competition at school a couple of months ago. Tough luck for you that you didn't get the big prize—a trip to Disney World and your story published in a national magazine."

"That's enough, Brayden and Jason!" Mrs. Hoffman said. "Instead of being mean to your sister, you should be complimenting her on her very mature attitude. We all make choices in life. Maddie's first choice is gymnastics, but that doesn't mean she will neglect her responsibilities, like getting her homework done. Playing basketball and football today and all day Saturday is your choice. I'm sure you will also act maturely and do your homework on Sunday without your father or I having to nag you. Right, Brayden?"

Mrs. Hoffman looked in the rearview mirror at Brayden. Suddenly speechless, Brayden just nodded his head so his mother could see that he agreed. But when she was no longer looking at him, Brayden stared down Maddie to show his anger. Despite his efforts to bother her, Maddie didn't seem to care. By the time they arrived home, Brayden's anger was gone, as all thoughts were now focused on the fun weekend ahead.

10.

THE BIG MISTAKE

Sunday morning arrived too quickly for the Hoffman triplets, but Maddie couldn't be happier. While Brayden, Rebecca, and Jason could not lift their heads from their pillows, Maddie was dressed and ready for practice at the crack of dawn. The hour and minute hands on the clock seemed to move at a snail's pace. When 9:00 AM finally arrived, Maddie was waiting impatiently by the garage door.

"Let's go, Dad! I don't want to be late for practice. I only have—"

"I know, Maddie," Dr. Hoffman said. "Just one week to go until the Meet." He smiled. "Let's go, Maddie Girl!"

When Maddie got to the gym, Katie was on the beam practicing her routine.

"What are you doing, Katie?" Maddie shouted. We need to warm up first. You know the rules. If Coach sees you..."

"Don't be a worrywart, Maddie," Katie responded. "Coach isn't here yet. I just wanted to get in a little extra time on the beam. I've got to make my routine perfect!"

"Your routine is already perfect! What happens if you get hurt?"

"I'm just about done," Katie answered. "Just my dismount and—"

THUMP! Katie fell to the floor.

"Oh no! My ankle, Maddie! I twisted it! I can't be hurt. What am I going to do?"

"I'll go get Coach. She'll know what to do," Maddie said.

"NO!" Katie shouted. "Don't tell her. She won't let me practice if she thinks I'm hurt. I'll be fine. I'll deal with the pain and suck it up. I'm not giving up."

"But what if your ankle is sprained? You could make it worse!" Maddie said, pleading with her friend.

"Coach Paul always tells Team they need to work through pain, so that's what I'm gonna do!"

"Paul is not our coach, Katie!"

"But Paul will be our coach if we make Team. Don't try to change my mind, Maddie. I know what I'm doing!"

Katie slowly got up from the mat. The look of pain on her face was intense.

"Please, Katie! You're hurt—"

"No, Maddie!" Katie said. "I'm fine, and you better not say anything to Coach. If you do, our friendship is over!"

As Katie walked slowly towards the warm-up mats, Maddie stared at her in shock. *What should I do?* she thought to herself. *If I tell Coach, I'll lose my best friend. If I don't tell, Katie could get hurt even more! But Mom always says that health comes before everything...no matter what! Katie isn't going to like this....*

"Let's go, Maddie!" Coach yelled. "You're late for warm-up, and we have a lot of work to do."

Maddie ran to the warm-up area. "I'm here, Coach, but I have to talk to you. It's important!"

"Later, Maddie. Start your running, girls, and use your arms!"

Maddie started running. As she pulled up next to Katie, she could see both pain and anger on her face. *Health before anything…no matter what!* Maddie repeated to herself.

"I'm sorry, Katie, but I have to tell Coach."

"Please, Maddie. Don't tell…"

THUD! Katie hit the floor again.

"Ouch!" Katie screamed. "My ankle! It hurts so much!"

"Oh no, Katie!" Maddie yelled. "I'm getting Coach right now!"

As Katie ran to get Coach, she shouted, "Help, Coach! Katie's hurt! Come quickly!"

Maddie and Coach ran back to Katie, where she was lying on the mat holding her ankle. Coach sat down next to her.

"What happened, Katie?" she asked.

"I hurt my ankle," she cried.

"I can see that, Katie, but why did you fall?" Coach asked. "Did you see what happened Maddie?"

Both girls looked at each other. Maddie knew she needed to tell Coach the truth, but just as she was about to confess, Katie stopped her.

"Wait, Maddie," Katie said quietly. "Let me tell her. It's all my fault."

With tears in her eyes and a cracking voice, Katie told Coach how she went on the beam before warm-up, hurt her ankle on dismount, and pretended nothing was wrong so she could continue to practice.

"I thought I could work through the pain, and it would go away. All I did was make it worse…and now I probably won't be able to try out for Team! How could I be so stupid?" Katie sobbed.

Coach Deb put her arms around Katie. "Slow down, Katie. Breathe. We don't know how badly you are hurt. You need to get checked by a doctor."

"Maddie, please get Katie a bag of ice and stay with her while I call her parents."

When Coach walked away, Maddie sat down next to Katie and took her hand.

"I'm so sorry, Maddie. I never should have said those mean things to you. I got so scared when I fell off the beam. It freaked me out. Will you forgive me and still be my best friend?"

"BFF's!" Maddie answered. "Team or no Team, we will be friends forever!"

❧

After Katie left, Coach Deb called all the girls together. "I know we are all very upset about Katie, so I think this is a good time to talk about the things we all need to do to avoid injury. What's the most important thing a gymnast can do to avoid getting hurt?"

"Conditioning!" the girls shouted in unison.

"Correct! And what are the three things that conditioning helps you to do?"

"I know!" Maya answered. "It warms our muscles; loosens joints like our knees, wrists, and ankles; and makes us focus better on our routines."

"Katie hurt her ankle," Jenny said. "That's a joint. Maybe if she'd warmed up, she wouldn't have gotten hurt."

"Maybe, Jenny," Coach Deb said. "I don't know for sure, but what I do know is that conditioning is very good for you and lessens your chances of getting hurt."

"Let's move on…. What have I said you must always do if you think you're hurt?"

"Call for help!" they all shouted.

"Yes! That's what your coaches are here for!"

"But Coach Paul always tells the girls on Team to work through the pain," Maddie said.

"I'm glad you brought that up," Coach Deb responded. "It's true that Coach Paul and other coaches tell gymnasts *to work through their pain*, but when they say this they aren't talking about those times when a gymnast gets hurt."

"So what are they talking about?" Jenny asked.

"Do you remember how you sometimes feel after you do new warm-up exercises and your muscles feel sore?"

"Oh yeah!" Maya said. "We all come to practice moaning and groaning."

"Right, Maya! And what might Coach Paul or I say to our students at warm-up time?"

"WORK THROUGH THE PAIN!" they shouted.

"Yes…just as long as we are sure that your moans or groans are just from sore muscles, it's okay to work out. But we don't say that unless we are positive you're not injured. Good coaches don't make this decision alone. We are a team, and who is on our team?"

"We are!" answered Maddie. "Each of us, our parents, and our coach."

"That's right, Maddie. We must always communicate with one another. Safety first!"

"My mom always says *Health comes before everything. No matter what!* That's why I wanted to tell you what happened to Katie, but I didn't get a chance."

"That's my fault, Maddie," Coach responded. "Next time one of you tells me you have something important to say, I promise I will listen right away. I've learned a lesson today, but I hope all of you have learned more than one."

"We know," said Jenny. "We must always warm up first, so we so we don't get hurt."

"And if we think we are hurt, we have to stop and ask for help," added Maya, "even if it turns out to be sore muscles."

"Exactly!" Coach said.

"But what about Katie? What's going to happen to her?" Maddie asked.

"I'm not sure right now. We're going to have to wait to hear what the doctor says. What I do know is that Katie made a big mistake today that has made all of us worried. But what do I always say about mistakes, girls?"

"Mistakes force us to change," they shouted, "and get better than before!"

11.

THE LONG WAIT

When Maddie returned home from practice on Sunday, she waited anxiously by the phone to find out what had happened to Katie. Neither watching TV nor listening to her favorite music on her headphones calmed her down. No matter what her parents tried to do to get her mind off Katie, Maddie wasn't interested. Even when her siblings offered to let her pick a movie to watch, she refused to do anything but sit in her room with her cellphone by her side. When her phone finally rang in the late afternoon, Maddie grabbed it.

"Katie, are you okay? What did the doctor say? Can you still be in the Meet?" Maddie said breathlessly.

On the other end of the phone, Katie said nothing. She had a lump in her throat that was so large it made her unable to speak.

"Katie, are you there? Talk to me! Tell me what happened!"

Taking a deep breath, Katie began to speak. "My ankle is sprained. I can't be in the Meet," Katie cried. "My foot is all swollen, and I have to wear a boot so my ankle doesn't move around. I can't believe this is happening to me! I should've listened to you. I'm so stupid."

"No you're not! You just made a mistake," Maddie said. "I'm sure you'll get better fast, and then you can come back to the gym."

"No! The doctor says I have to be all healed before I come back. I wish I could be there, but my parents and Coach won't let me. If I were on Team, I bet Coach Paul would let me. I always see lots of girls from Team practicing after they've been injured."

"But that's not a good idea," said Maddie. "Remember last year when Emily sprained her wrist and then broke it because she came back too soon? She was out the entire year!"

"I guess you're right. I just want to be at the gym…with you…at the Meet…trying out for Team!"

Maddie didn't know what to say. She knew how she'd feel if it had happened to her. Just as she was about to try and make her feel better, Katie continued speaking.

"I guess I have to be patient. Coach Deb spoke to Coach Paul, and they agreed that I can try out for Team after my ankle heals and I do lots of rehab exercise. But Mom says I can go to the Meet to cheer on my best friend." Katie hesitated and swallowed hard. "Gotta go, Maddie. See you Sunday."

12.

MADDIE

I never thought trying out for Team would be so hard! First, I had to deal with Maya and Jenny being mean to me, and now Katie sprained her ankle and can't be in the Meet. I know I should feel happy that Katie will be able to try out when her ankle heals, but it's just not the same without her. I haven't been able to focus, and this is the last week before the Meet!

When I went to the gym on Tuesday and Thursday, I was okay during warm-up and group practice, but I kept messing up my routine. I don't know why this was happening. I did just what Coach Deb has taught us to do. I closed my eyes, took a deep breath, and tried to visualize all the steps of my routine, but the only thing I could see and hear was Katie falling. By the end of practice on Thursday, I was a mess. I actually started to cry, and I never cry because I'm tough. Well...maybe not so tough. I do cry, but I don't let others see me.

So I wiped away my tears and tried to get myself to concentrate. I started talking to myself like Coach Deb has shown us. She calls it "positive self-talk." That means we need to say things that will make us feel good about ourselves. I was trying to do that when Coach walked up to me. I thought she hadn't seen me crying, but she had. She also knew I had messed up my routine. I was sure she was going to tell me that I couldn't try out for Team because I wasn't ready. But she didn't! She told me I was messing up because I was thinking about Katie. It's like she was reading my mind!

After we talked for a while, I was able to get back on focus. When I closed my eyes before I started my routine again, the picture and sounds of Katie falling disappeared. Right in front of me were all the moves I needed to make in my routine. It was amazing! All of a sudden I was back on track and did my routine without mistakes! Now I have to make sure that everything goes perfectly tomorrow when it really counts. I'm not going to say "Wish me Luck" this time because luck isn't gonna get me on Team. I'm the only one who can do that, and I'm ready!

46

What Do You Think?

What will happen when Maddie goes to the Spring All Around Meet on Sunday? (Place an "X" next to your prediction below.)

☐ Maddie will do her routine perfectly and make Team.

☐ Maddie will mess up her routine and will not be allowed to join Team.

☐ Other: _____

Explain why you made your prediction above:

_____

_____

_____

_____

_____

_____

_____

_____

_____

_____

_____

13.

SUNDAY MORNING PREP

Sunday morning arrived, and once again Maddie was up at the crack of dawn. This time, however, she wasn't waiting for her parents or her siblings to awaken. It was time for the entire Hoffman family to get up so she wouldn't be late for the biggest day of her life.

Upstairs, Maddie opened the bedroom doors of each of her siblings, yelled at them to get out of bed, and ran downstairs to make sure her parents were up, too.

"Mom! Dad!" she shouted. "Get up! Everybody has to be ready! I have to be at the gym by 9:00 AM. You've got to get Brayden, Rebecca, and Jason up, too. I can't be late!"

As Dr. Hoffman stretched his arms, he said, "Not to worry, Maddie Girl. I'm going to drop you off right on time, and Mom will bring your brothers and sister before the Meet starts at 10:00. We've got everything covered."

As Maddie moved to the other side of her parents' bed, where Mrs. Hoffman was still dozing, she pulled on her arm. "Mom, you need to get up right now. I need your help with my hair. It has to be perfect!" Maddie pleaded.

"Okay, Maddie," Mrs. Hoffman said, yawning. "I'll be right there. Go get breakfast. Remember you need to eat lightly—whole wheat toast, yogurt, and a banana…"

"I know that!" Maddie shouted, as she ran towards the kitchen. "Coach said we can't eat too much right before the Meet. I'll take some energy bars for later on."

After breakfast, Maddie put on her Superstars royal blue leotard with white stars. Imprinted with the initials "HSG" for the Harrison Street Gym, she loved the way the crystals on the stars and letters sparkled. Finding her matching sparkly blue scrunchie, Maddie ran out of her room to shout for her mother.

"Mom," she yelled from the top of the stairwell. "Where are—"

But Maddie didn't get a chance to finish. Her mother was right there walking up the stairs with comb, gel, and bobby pins in her hands.

"Let's do this, Maddie!"

Maddie returned to her room and sat down on her white wicker desk chair so her mother could do her hair.

"Just make a simple bun, Mom. It's the fastest one to make. I've got to get to the gym!"

"Yes, Maddie. I know." Mrs. Hoffman laughed to herself, not wanting Maddie to think she was making fun of her. She then quickly gelled Maddie's hair and combed it into a high ponytail. With an elastic band in place, Mrs. Hoffman wrapped Maddie's hair around the base of the ponytail and secured it with lots of bobby pins. She knew you could never have enough of them when doing gymnastics. The blue scrunchie was the final touch.

"You look perfect, Maddie. Just like a real superstar!" Mrs. Hoffman beamed. "But I think something is missing..."

"What do you mean?" Maddie said quickly. "I have everything I need right here in my gym bag—towel, comb, hair brush, bobby pins, power bars..."

"No, Maddie," Mrs. Hoffman said, interrupting. "I'm not talking about your gym supplies. I'm talking about something very special."

"Yes! Very special for a very special person, Maddie Girl," Dr. Hoffman added, as he walked into Maddie's room.

Maddie was clueless. She had no idea what her parents were talking about and could only think of one thing—getting to the gym on time. Just as she was about to tell her father they needed to leave, her mother reached into her pocket and pulled out the most beautiful necklace she had ever seen! A sapphire blue five-pointed star set in the middle of a shiny silver chain glistened in her mother's hands.

"This is for you, Maddie," Mrs. Hoffman said. "At the Harrison Street Gym, you're a Superstar, but to us, you're always be a star no matter what you do or where you are!" Her mother then handed Maddie the necklace.

"Wow! It's so beautiful! I love it. Thank you!"

"I know you can't wear it at the gym, but it will be here waiting for you when you come home," Mrs. Hoffman said.

As Maddie gently placed the necklace in the pretty blue velvet box Mom handed her, Dr. Hoffman said, "We're so proud of you, Maddie Girl. Now let's go so we're not late!"

Maddie quickly put her new treasure in her jewelry box, grabbed her gym bag, and ran down the stairs. "Let's go, Dad. Your Maddie Girl is ready to rock!"

14.

THE SPRING ALL AROUND MEET

M addie got to the gym at 9:00 AM on the dot. With not
a minute to spare, she gave her father a quick hug and
ran off to begin her warm-up. *One hour to go,* she thought
to herself impatiently, but then she tried to think positively.
*No! I'm not gonna watch the clock. Coach says to enjoy every
moment. So that's what I'm going to do!*

When warm-up ended, Coach gathered the girls together
for a pep talk before the Meet began. Even Katie was there.
Although she couldn't participate, Coach wanted her to be
together with the group throughout the Meet.

"Girls...I have never been prouder of you than I am right
now. You are the finest Advanced group I have ever taught!
Not only have you mastered your skills, but you have also
shown teamwork and sportsmanship. Now go out on that
floor, have fun, and make us proud. But most of all, make
yourself proud! You are Superstars!"

ॐ

With Coach Deb's final words, the lights dimmed and
the Spring All Around Meet began. Maddie and her class
sat on the sidelines for the first hour while the Superstars

Beginner and Intermediate Recreational Classes performed their special routines. This was followed by coaches giving out certificates to all gymnasts for the highest color completed in the Superstars program.

Maddie tried to be patient, but she was just too excited. She knew that when the final names were read, it would be her turn. It was the moment she had been waiting for—her tryout for TEAM and USA Gymnastics. Just when she thought she couldn't wait any longer, Coach Deb stepped up to the microphone.

"And now, it's time for our tryouts where gymnasts in our Superstars Advanced Recreational Class get the chance to try out for Team if they have earned their seventh and final star—the GOLD! We have two students who have qualified—Katie Fisher and Maddie Hoffman."

Applause and cheers echoed throughout the gym. When the crowd settled down, Coach continued.

"Unfortunately, Katie can't try out today because she sprained her ankle, but don't worry! Katie will get her chance the minute her ankle is healed."

"Katie! Katie! Katie!" the audience cheered.

Maddie squeezed Katie's hand. "Listen! They're cheering for you."

"I know! I can't believe it!" Katie said. "But it's your turn now. Just go out there and do it, Maddie. Make yourself proud, just like Coach said."

Before Maddie could respond, Coach Deb was announcing her name. "I now present to you, Maddie Hoffman!"

As she walked to the floor, the cheers started again. Maddie got into position and waited for the crowd to settle down. She took a deep breath, closed her eyes, and visualized every movement of her compulsory routine. When her intro music began, Maddie was ready. Starting off with a *straddle jump,* she moved quickly through each skill—*front handspring, back extension roll, split leap, back walkover, round-off back handspring,* and *back tuck.* When she finished her routine, she couldn't believe it was over. Everyone in the audience started clapping and shouting her name, just like they had for Katie.

"Maddie! Maddie! Maddie!"

Maddie was so happy. The audience loved her performance. While the crowd continued to cheer, however, Maddie couldn't help but think about the coaches who were judging her. *Was I good enough to make Team? How many mistakes did I make?*

Maddie's thoughts were interrupted when Coach Deb approached the microphone to announce her group's finale presentation. Maddie realized she needed to refocus. *I can't think about Team now! The girls are waiting for me. I can do this! Coach said to have fun. That means right now!*

૰

And Maddie did have fun! All the Advanced Superstars had a blast. Their spectacular finale was greeted with cheers and a standing ovation from everyone in the audience. The girls were so proud of themselves! After Coach distributed their Superstars certificates, they all hugged and gave each other high fives.

With the Meet now over, the audience gathered their belongings and left the gym. As the Hoffmans walked out, Jason asked Brayden, "Do you think Maddie will make Team?"

"I don't know," Brayden responded. "She made a bunch of mistakes."

"How would you know if she made any mistakes?" Rebecca asked. "You know nothing about gymnastics!"

"Enough!" Mrs. Hoffman said, scolding them. "Whatever happens, we are going to act like a team and be there for Maddie. That's what Hoffmans do! Go get in the car. Dad will wait for Maddie."

"Why can't we all wait to hear what happens?" Jason asked. "You said we are a team. Shouldn't we stick together?"

"Yes, Jason. You're right. We are a team, but in this case, Maddie needs to hear the news without her entire family. Since we don't know what the decision will be, it will be easier for her to hear it with just Dad by her side. Afterwards, we will be there for her no matter what happens. Let's go home."

❧

Maddie waited on the bench outside the locker room. Although her father sat right next to her with his arm around her shoulder, she could not stop shaking.

"What's taking so long?" Maddie asked. "Maybe they're having a hard time deciding because I made too many mistakes."

"Maddie, you were terrific!" Dr. Hoffman said. "Try to relax."

"How can I relax when my whole life depends on the decision the coaches make?" Maddie shouted.

Just as Dr. Hoffman was about to answer, Coach Deb and Coach Paul walked out of the office. Maddie jumped up and ran over to them.

"Coach Deb! Coach Paul! Did I make Team? Please tell me!" Maddie pleaded.

Coach Deb and Coach Paul looked at each other and then at Maddie. Thinking she was about to get the bad news she didn't want to hear, Maddie turned her head away so they couldn't see the tears forming in her eyes.

"Maddie," Coach Deb said gently. "We have something I think you're going to want to see."

Maddie quickly wiped away her tears and turned back to face them. When she looked down at what Coach Paul was holding, she couldn't believe her eyes—the Harrison Street Gym's **TEAM** t-shirt!

"This is for you, Maddie," Coach Paul announced. "Welcome to Team!"

Holding her Team t-shirt tightly in her hands, all she could think about was that she'd finally made it! "I did it!" she blurted out, as she hugged her father.

"Yes, you did, Maddie Girl," Dr. Hoffman said proudly.

"We're going to miss you in our Rec class," Coach Deb said, "but you're ready to move on. Congratulations!"

After Maddie gave Coach Deb a big hug, Coach Paul got down to business.

"Team practice is Monday, Wednesday, and Friday at 4:00 PM. See you tomorrow, and be on time!"

Maddie smiled at her father and then looked back at her new coach. "No problem, Coach Paul. Maddie Hoffman is always on time!"

With her gym bag in one hand and her new Team t-shirt in the other, Maddie and her father left the gym. As they got into the car, Maddie was already on Dad's cell phone shouting her big news to her mother and siblings.

"I just can't believe this is happening to me!" Maddie exclaimed.

"Believe it, Maddie Girl! You made it happen," Dr. Hoffman said.

"We're so proud of you!" Mrs. Hoffman added. The minute you get home, we're going to celebrate."

"Maddie! Maddie! Maddie!" the triplets shouted. "Let's get this party going! Hoffmans rock!"

15.

MADDIE

*T*EAM! *I still can't believe it! At first I had to pinch myself to make sure it wasn't just a dream, but now I know it's for real. I just finished two full weeks of workouts, and just like Coach Deb said, "this is the BIG TIME!"*

I'm at the gym nine hours during the school week and four hours on the weekend. When I'm not practicing, I have to get all my homework done. It's not so bad on the weekends, but during the week, it's really hard to do it all.

But I'm not gonna complain because Maddie Hoffman is not a quitter! Every time I think things might be getting too much for me, I put my hands on my shiny sapphire blue star necklace and remember that Mom and Dad are always there for me. And sometimes so are Brayden, Rebecca, and Jason. I can't believe they haven't been giving me a hard time! So how can I lose knowing that I have Team Hoffman on my side? I'm just going to enjoy every moment like Coach Deb says and have lots of fun. What could be better than that?

Signing off!
Maddie

Prediction Check-up
What were your predictions? Were they correct?

Question	Your Prediction	Correct or Incorrect
1. What did you think would happen when Maddie confronted Maya and Jenny after they made fun of her?		
2. Did you think that Maddie or Katie would make any mistakes before the meet?		
3. Did you think Maddie would make Team?		

What Should Have Happened?
Would you have liked this novel to end in a different way? If so, how?

_____

_____

_____

_____

Share your predictions, comments, or questions with the author.

Write to Diane Wander at:
tripletroubleplusone@gmail.com

Maddie's Gymnastics Glossary

All-Around
A category of gymnastics that includes all events—floor, beam, bars, and vault

Apparatus
Equipment used in gymnastics, such as the balance beam, floor, uneven bars, and vault

Back extension roll
A back roll with a push to a vertical handstand with legs together

Back handspring
A tumbling move where a gymnast takes off from one or two feet, jumps backward onto the hands, and lands on the feet

Back tuck
Usually done from a back handspring, with the gymnast stretching their arms upward overhead, while at the same time, jumping upward with the legs; also called a backward somersault

Balance beam
One of the four apparatus used in gymnastics where gymnasts perform a series of connected skills on a four-inch-wide wooden platform while trying to keep their balance

Bun
A hairstyle often worn during gymnastic competitions in which the hair is drawn back into a tight coil at the back of the head

Cartwheel
A movement where the body turns over sideways with the arms and legs spread out; can be done on the floor, beam, or vault runway

Competition
An event where a group of gymnasts, usually all in the same level, do routines, get judged, and get placed gold, silver, bronze, etc.

Conditioning
Exercises gymnasts do to warm-up and strengthen their muscles and loosen joints

Deductions
Errors that cause gymnasts to lose points from their score; e.g., stepping out of bounds on the floor exercise

Dismount
Getting off an apparatus such as the balance beam at the end of a routine

Element

A single move that is scored in a gymnastic performance

Floor

One of the four apparatus in gymnastics, which is used for tumbling and dance

Front Handspring

A tumbling move in which gymnasts take a running start, then place their hands down as if doing a handstand, kick one leg over, push off the ground, and come back up

Gymnast

A person who does gymnastics

Gymnastics

A sport in which exercises are done on floor, the balance beam, uneven bars, and vault

- Competitive gymnastics—for gymnasts who have been invited to join a team after being evaluated by a coach
- Recreational gymnastics—for gymnasts who want to improve their gymnastic skills but are not members of a team

Handstand

A movement where the body is balanced on the hands and the feet are in the air, with the legs together or in a straddle or split position

Joints
Parts of the body that hold the skeleton together; e.g., ankles, elbows, knees

Meet
Another word for a gymnastics competition

Muscles
Parts of the body that move the bones of the skeleton

Positive Self-talk
Talking to yourself aloud or silently to make yourself feel better about what you have done or are going to do

Rehab or Rehabilitation
Treatment given to a gymnast after an injury to help the body get better

Rep
A shortened version of repetition; one cycle of the action or motion being done in a gymnastics exercise

Rotation
The order in which gymnasts move from one apparatus to another in a competition

Round-off
A move similar to a cartwheel except the gymnast lands with two feet placed together on the ground instead of one foot at a time

Round-off back handspring
A back handspring that is done after a round-off, which helps the gymnast do a faster and more powerful handspring

Routine (compulsory and optional)
A combination of skills and dance moves, sometimes performed to music, on an apparatus such as the balance beam, bars, and floor

- A compulsory routine—one where all gymnasts perform the same set of skills in the same order
- An optional routine—one where a gymnast has a set of skills from which to choose but selects the music she likes and the skills she wants to display in order to show her strengths

Scrunchie
A circular band of fabric-covered elastic used by gymnasts to fasten hair into a ponytail or bun

Side handstand
An advanced type of handstand done on the balance beam in which the body faces away from the beam as you do the handstand

Split
A stretching position of the legs with one leg stretched in front of the body and one leg stretched behind the body; legs parallel to the floor and straight without any bend to the knees when done correctly

Split Jump (also called Split Leap)
A sequence of body movements in which a gymnast does a split after leaping or jumping from the floor while still in the air

Straddle jump
A jump where one leg is extended to the left side of the body and the other leg is extended to the right side; correct when legs are straight without a bend to the knees

Trick
A movement or skill in a gymnastic routine

Tumbling
A series of connected movements that usually involve air time (ex., round-off back handspring back tuck)

Uneven bars
One of the four apparatus used in gymnastics where the gymnast moves between bars performing connected tricks while trying not to fall

USA Gymnastics
The governing body of gymnastics in the United States

Vault
One of the four apparatus (also called horse) used in gymnastics where the gymnast does a series of tricks leading up to and flying over the vault

Walkover (front and back)
A move used on the floor and balance beam with the gymnast starting in a standing position, walking into a handstand position, continuing into a backbend and finishing in a standing position; performed in either the forward or backward direction

Warm-up
The beginning of a training session when gymnasts exercise their muscles so they don't injure themselves while training

THANK YOU NOTES

❦First I want to thank my four children—Benjamin Wander, Robin Sherman, Joshua Wander, and Mollie Wander—who are now all adults. *Maddie Hoffman Gymnastics Superstar* and my first book *Triple Trouble Plus One* would not exist without them. Although these novels are works of fiction, the personalities of the Hoffman foursome are based on my own triplets plus one more when they were children.

❦I especially want to thank Mollie, as she was the inspiration for this second novel in the *Triple Trouble Plus One* series. Her love of gymnastics as a child motivated me to learn more about this sport and then write another novel. Mollie's advice along the way was so helpful in making this book the story it finally came to be.

❦Thank you to Jo Ann Laskin and Sandra Friedman, two close friends and colleagues, who provided their educators' expertise after reading the first draft of *Maddie Hoffman Gymnastics Superstar*. I'm so appreciative of all their advice with this novel, as well as with *Triple Trouble Plus One*.

❦I am so grateful to my mentor, Ellen Brazer, published author of two novels and one non-fiction book. Ellen was kind enough to sit with me and read aloud one of my first drafts of

Maddie Hoffman Gymnastics Superstar. Words can not express how thankful I am to Ellen for all her guidance with both my novels. My growing confidence as a writer is largely due to her!

&What would this book have been without advice from students! Thank you to my volunteer group of students, who read my book and then completed a "Book Critic Response Log." Their feedback was so helpful!

- Raquel Zajac (grade 5) and Natalie Levinson (grade 6) of the Scheck Hillel Community School in North Miami Beach, Florida
- Mia Finvarb (grade 5) of the Lehrman Community School in Miami Beach, Florida

&This book wouldn't have been written without help from gymnasts themselves. I was so fortunate to have a number of student gymnasts who agreed to be interviewed. Thank you to:

- Natalie Levinson—a grade 6 gymnast at the JCC Miami Beach, Florida
- Mia Finvarb—a grade 5 gymnast at MIA Dance Factory in Miami Beach, Florida
- Rachel Hegarty—a grade 6 gymnast at Progressive Gymnastics in New Hyde Park, NY
- Sophie Mooallem—a grade 6 gymnast at Gymnastics Revolution in Riviera Beach, Florida
- Selected students from the 2015–2016 Grade 5 Girls Book Club at Torah Academy in Boca Raton, Florida, who have attended a variety of gymnastic programs in Palm Beach County.

❧A very special thanks to Coach Samantha Nelson of the Park Avenue Gym, who gave me the opportunity to interview her and observe one of her gymnastics classes at the Park Avenue Gym in Cooper City, Florida. Having a front row seat to an actual gymnastics class made the writing of a number of chapters of my novel so much easier!

❧As many times as an author revises and edits an novel, it is never enough. Professional advice is always needed. I am fortunate that I was able to turn to Integrative Ink Editing and Publishing Services, who added the final touch with their superb editing, book design, and layout of this novel. Thank you to Editor Stephanee Killen for her time, effort, and professional expertise.

❧Finally, I would like to thank my husband Stephen. It was so comforting to know you were always there to provide encouragement and advice as I wrote every chapter. Just like Team Hoffman, I am so fortunate to always have Team Wander—you and our four children—always by my side. Lots of love and thanks to all of you!

ABOUT THE ILLUSTRATORS

RAQUEL ZAJAC is a ten year old girl who attends fifth grade at the Scheck Community School in North Miami Beach, Florida. As she loves to write and draw, her dream has always been to illustrate a book. Raquel's dream came true with the publishing of *Triple Trouble Plus One*. Not only did Raquel create many of the images for the author's first novel but she has made some of the interior illustrations in *Maddie Hoffman Gymnastics Superstar*.

LEDA ALMAR is an Argentinian artist and illustrator. She has lived in Weston, Florida since 2000 where she has a private studio in which she works and teaches drawing, painting, and ceramics. In addition to *Triple Trouble Plus One* and now *Maddie Hoffman Gymnastics Superstar*, Ms. Almar has illustrated the books of several Argentinian authors.

CPSIA information can be obtained
at www.ICGtesting.com
Printed in the USA
BVOW03s1046160417
481396BV00001B/67/P

TRIPLE TROUBLE PLUS ONE

BOOK 2

MADDIE HOFFMAN GYMNASTICS SUPERSTAR

by
Diane Wander